Stan Has a Plan

By
Daniel Rivers

MAPLE
PUBLISHERS

Stan Has a Plan

Author: Daniel Rivers

Copyright © Daniel Rivers

The right of Daniel Rivers to be identified as author of this work has been asserted by the author in accordance with section 77 and 78 of the Copyright, Designs and Patents Act 1988.

First Published in 2024

ISBN 978-1-83538-042-0 (Paperback)
   978-1-83538-043-7 (E-Book)

Cover, Illustrations, and Book Layout by:
   White Magic Studios
   www.whitemagicstudios.co.uk

Published by:
   Maple Publishers
   Fairbourne Drive, Atterbury,
   Milton Keynes,
   MK10 9RG, UK
   www.maplepublishers.com

A CIP catalogue record for this title is available from the British Library.

A long time ago
in a far distant place,
lived an old rabbit called Stan,
who loved the slow pace.

Stan's home in a field
was a large secret passage,
and he loved to fill it
with carrots and cabbage.

He moved when he had to.
This was his choosing,
to have a life that was full
of snacking and snoozing.

Despite his older age,
friendship never ended.
When his pals were in trouble,
it's them he defended.

Brave and respected,
loved and admired,
so when bad ones threatened,
his help was required.

One evening, he heard a sound,
that caused some alarm.
It was a rooster called Ronnie
from Fenswick Farm.

Cock a Doodle Doo

Cock a Doodle Doo

Fenswick Farm

He put on his straw hat,
and made a selection
of which carrot he should take
from his private collection.

Off he went to his destination
leaving behind his burrow.
He pondered what could be wrong
whilst walking through the meadow.

At the farm, Ronnie sobbed,
"There's a hole in our fence.
A nasty wolf called Clive
is causing offence.

"He approached the boundary.
The beast gave us a fright.
He said that he will have us all
for a feast tonight."

"Help us, Stan!" he squawked,
"do something, please!"
All the animals could see
the knocking of Ronnie's knees.

Fenswick Farm

Stan tried to think of a plan
then snapped his paws.
He had an idea
that was worthy of applause.

After grouping the animals together,
Stan whispered his plan to all.
Each of them loved it,
from the beetle to the bull.

A special task in mind
for Dolly the sheep.
They discussed it in depth
before getting some sleep.

A short nap to refresh,
then the animals awoke.
They knew what to do,
so nobody spoke.

Shortly before midnight,
Clive crept to the hole.
A monsterous wolf
as big as a troll.

Clive quietly salivated
while he thought of him chewing
a mouse, a cockerel
and a sheep good for stewing.

He sniggered to himself,
then made not a sound.
Assuming all asleep,
into the farm went the hound.

Finally, he took
a deep breath of air.
It was dinner time, he thought
with a menacing glare.

He approached the old oak,
and stopped dead in his tracks.
Sid the Squirrel was hanging
in what looked like a sack.

As he got closer,
he heard Sid shout out,
"Spider! Help me!
There's a spider about."

Spiders were Clive's
only main fear.
Small ones were fine
as long as large ones weren't near.

He saw creature after creature,
and his eyes grew wider.
They were all wrapped in something
like the web of a spider.

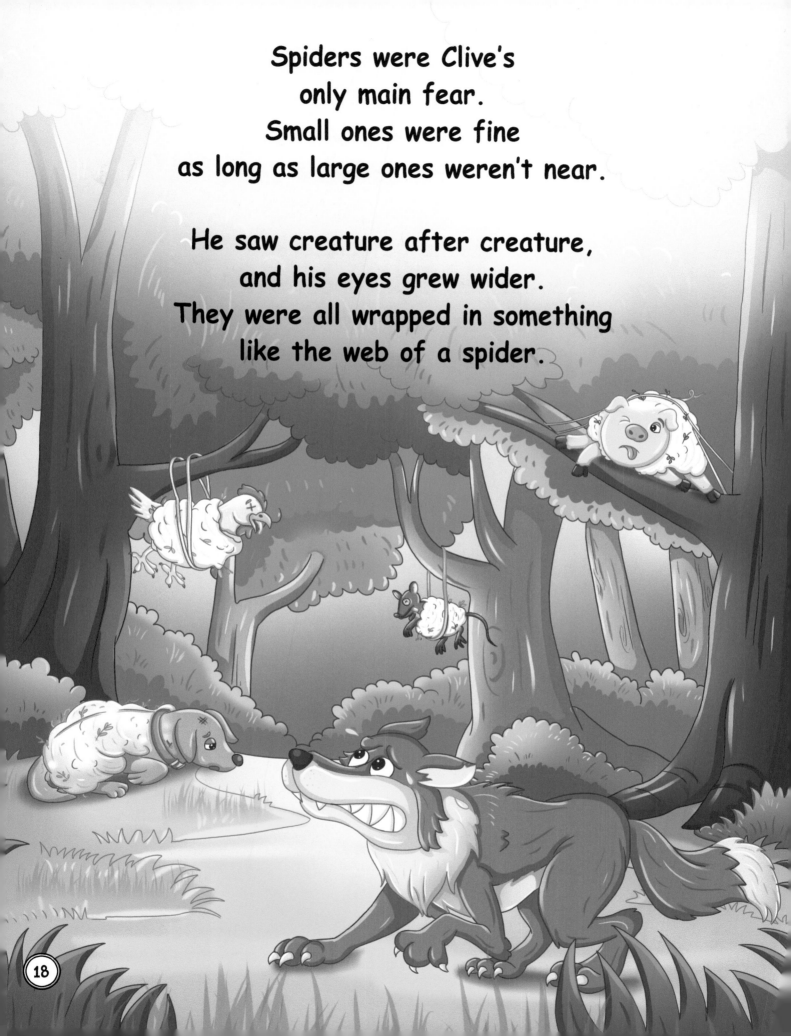

Clive now looked up
as his senses were heightened.
He heard Ronnie shrieking
like he'd been frightened.

He was flapping about
making the most terrible sound.
Clive was wishing
he'd never come round.

Suddenly, out of the hen house
came a dark figure.
As it got closer,
it looked meaner and bigger.

He counted eight legs;
this was no longer a laugh.
His own legs wobbled
like a baby giraffe.

The spider was still,
whilst it counted to five.
Suddenly it ran
straight toward Clive.

He let out a scream,
and his eyes filled with dread.
As quick as a flash,
he then turned and fled.

Cheers could be heard
from far and wide.
The animals unwrapped wool
that each had applied.

In the dark, from a distance,
and to an outsider,
Dolly's wool looked like
the web from a spider.

All of the animals
(Stan himself included)
bounded over to the sheep
where everyone concluded...

Dolly actually did look like
a spider indeed.
She was head to hoof
in thick mud and reeds.

They all fell about laughing
then Ronnie declared,
"Thank you Stan, what a great idea!
The big beast was so scared.

"How will we ever repay you?"
Ronnie continued.
"A cabbage and a carrot
is all I need issued."

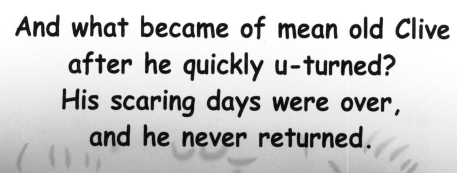

And what became of mean old Clive
after he quickly u-turned?
His scaring days were over,
and he never returned.

Milton Keynes UK
Ingram Content Group UK Ltd.
UKHW050014310824
447644UK00002B/17